SOPHIE the HERO

☆

Finding the right name isn't easy!
See what else Sophie tries out. . . .

1: SOPHIE the AWESOME

2: SOPHIE the HERO

3: SOPHIE the CHATTERBOX

4: SOPHIE the ZILLIONAIRE

4: SOPHIE the SNOOP

SOPHIE
the HERO

by Lara Bergen

illustrated by Laura Tallardy

SCHOLASTIC INC.

New York Toronto London Auckland
Sydney Mexico City New Delhi Hong Kong

ISBN 978-0-545-14605-0

Text copyright © 2010 by Lara Bergen.
Illustrations copyright © 2010 by Scholastic Inc.
All rights reserved. Published by Scholastic Inc.
SCHOLASTIC, LITTLE APPLE, and associated logos are trademarks
and/or registered trademarks of Scholastic Inc.

12 11 10 9 8 7 6 5 4 3   10 11 12 13 14 15/0

Printed in the U.S.A.   40
First printing, July 2010
Designed by Tim Hall

To my heroes, Parker and Sydney

CHAPTER 1

Sophie was a hero. No joke. A real live hero! And it was all anyone could talk about on the bus to school.

Especially Sophie.

"Mrs. Blatt! Have you heard? I'm a hero!" she told the bus driver as soon as she got on. "Just call me Sophie the Hero from now on! Right, Ella?"

She turned to Ella Fitzgibbon, the little kindergartner behind her.

"Right!" said Ella. "Sophie the Hero — my hero!"

Sophie smiled. Then she patted Ella's head. This was something the old, boring Sophie never would have done. But she was not the old, boring Sophie anymore.

The old, boring Sophie had thought that her next-door neighbor Ella was a pest. She never left Sophie alone, even when Sophie was playing important *third-grade* games with Kate Barry, her very best friend.

But things had changed. Now Sophie was Ella's hero! And thanks to Ella, Sophie had a great new name. A name that made her special. A name that said it all—just what Sophie had been hoping for!

So what if it was not "Sophie the Awesome"? That was the name she had first thought of. But being awesome all the time was kind of hard, Sophie had learned. Being a hero was fine with her. Great, even!

"Hero?" Mrs. Blatt said. She reached over and closed the bus door. "You don't say! Well, have a seat, girls, and tell me more. On your bottoms back there!" she hollered to the kids in the rear of the bus.

Quickly, Sophie, Kate, and Ella slid into the first seat behind Mrs. Blatt. Usually, Sophie liked to sit in the back of the bus with Kate. Not with Ella. But this was not a usual day. Ella had already told Sophie's story at the bus stop, to all the kids who had missed it. And Sophie could not wait to hear it again!

"Go ahead, Ella," Sophie said.

"What happened," Ella said, "is that I tripped and all my Slinkys spilled. Right into the street!"

"And Sophie caught them all?" said the bus driver. She hit the gas and the bus rolled forward. "Why, that *is* heroic, isn't it?"

But all three girls shook their heads.

"No. Sophie caught *Ella!*" Kate said. She patted Sophie's shoulder proudly.

"I was going to try to catch my Slinkys. But Sophie stopped me from running into the street," Ella said.

"And don't forget the part about Mrs. Dixon

driving by in her car right then," Sophie reminded them.

"Right!" said Ella. "And Mrs. Dixon drove by in her car! Right then!" She turned to Sophie and hugged her hard. "You saved my life!"

Mrs. Blatt's eyes grew wide in the rearview mirror. "Wow, Sophie. You really are a hero!"

Sophie beamed proudly as Ella reached down and pulled a piece of paper out of her backpack. She handed it to Sophie. It was a drawing of a girl with two straight lines of brown hair. She was standing on a line of green grass with heart-shaped flowers all around her. There was a line of blue sky above, a yellow sun in the corner, and big rainbow letters that spelled out "SOFEE THE HE."

Sophie *started* to smile, but her mouth ended up crooked. And not just because the picture made her look like a scarecrow wearing too much makeup.

"This isn't what I told you to write, Ella," Sophie said, pointing to the letters on the paper.

"Oh, I ran out of room," Ella said. She grinned. "The rest is on the back."

Sophie turned the page over. There was a giant *R*, and an *O*. Plus an "I love you, Ella. XXXOOO."

"See!" said Ella. She looked at Sophie with big brown eyes. Sophie noticed a spot of purple jelly on her chin. "Don't you like it?" Ella asked her.

Sophie sighed.

"I think it's great," Kate said. She smiled at Sophie over Ella's head. "And it looks just like you, Sophie... the *He!*"

Sophie rolled her eyes, but she had to grin.

"It's... very nice, Ella," she said.

Then she slipped the picture into her own backpack. Okay. So it was not exactly the hero portrait she had hoped for. But Sophie did not need a picture to prove she was a hero. The facts spoke for themselves. And so did the cheer that Kate and Ella started on the bus ride:

Two, four, six, eight, who do we appreciate?
Sophie!

5

Sophie!

Sophie the Hero!

☆   ☆   ☆

At school, Sophie dropped Ella off at her kindergarten classroom. (Ella clung to her arm the whole way there, which was kind of cute...and kind of not.) Then she and Kate hurried to their third-grade class in room 10.

Sophie was just about to walk through the door when she stopped short.

"Oof!" grunted Kate as she bumped into Sophie's backpack. "Why did you stop here?"

Sophie pulled Kate away from the door. "You need to introduce me!" she told her.

Kate's forehead made a wrinkle. "But everybody already knows you," she said.

Sophie lowered her voice. "Not as Sophie the Hero," she said.

"Oh, right!" Kate waggled her eyebrows and grinned. Then, slowly, her grin got smaller.

"What?" Sophie asked.

"Well...," Kate began. She shrugged. "It's

6

just . . . it's great that you're a hero. But I feel a little left out."

"Oh, don't!" Sophie said. She put her hands on her friend's shoulders. She had never thought that her being a hero would be hard for Kate.

"Don't forget," Sophie told her, "you're the *best friend* of a hero. In fact—" A thought suddenly hit her. "You're like my . . . What do they call them?"

"Sidekick?" said Kate.

Sophie beamed. "Exactly! You're like my sidekick!" And how perfect was that? Every hero needed one of them!

Kate thought about it for a second and her grin came back even bigger.

"Feel better?" said Sophie.

"Much better!" Kate said. "Sidekicks get the coolest jobs, and they're funny, like me. Now for that introduction!"

With that, Kate left Sophie in the hall and stepped into room 10.

"Ladies and gentlemen! And everyone else, too," Kate declared. (Sophie bet she was talking to yucky Toby Myers and Archie Dolan.) "May I have your attention, please?"

Sophie heard the class get quiet, no kidding. Wow! How lucky was she to have Kate for a sidekick? Kate was very good at it already!

"What is it?" someone said.

That was when Kate grabbed Sophie and pulled her into the room.

"I'd like you to meet the one, the only . . . Sophie the Hero!" Kate cried.

"Sophie the who?"

"Sophie the what?"

Sophie took a bow and cleared her throat. "Sophie the Hero," she said.

And just as Sophie had hoped, she and Kate got to tell the Slinky story all over again.

And again!

"Wow, you *are* a hero!" said Eve, Mia, Sydney, and Grace when it was over.

"Maybe we should call you Sophie H. instead of Sophie M.," said Sophie A., the other Sophie in her class. "For 'Sophie the Hero.'"

Sophie thought about it for a second, then shook her head. No. "Sophie the Hero" was better. She was pretty sure of that.

"I am happy to sign autographs," Sophie said. "Does anyone have a pen?"

"Wait a minute," said a snooty voice. It belonged to Mindy VonBoffmann. Her name would be Mindy the Meanie if Sophie had anything to say about it.

"What happened to the Slinkys?" Mindy asked.

Sophie shrugged. "Mrs. Dixon picked them up."

"Then isn't *she* the real hero?" Mindy said. She crossed her arms and made a face that Sophie's mom would have called sassy.

"Yeah," Lily Lemley chimed in. She liked to copy Mindy, so she made her face look just the same. "If Mrs. Dixon saved the Slinkys, she's the real hero," Lily said.

"What are you talking about?" Kate said. "Sophie saved a kindergartner! Who cares about the Slinkys?"

"They only cost a dollar or something," Ben added. "Kindergartners cost a lot more."

Good old Ben. Sophie turned to smile at him.

She truly felt like a hero. And that felt really good!

But Mindy just shrugged. "I guess," she said. "Still, it's only one kindergartner. It's not like she saved five kittens from a burning building, like Scarlett the cat. Remember? Now, that's a real hero."

"Yeah, that's a real hero," Lily echoed.

Sophie remembered the story their second-grade teacher, Mrs. Cruz, had read to them the year before. It was a true story about a stray cat who saved the lives of all her kittens. When the building they lived in caught fire, she carried them out, one by one.

Okay. Yes. Sophie knew that the cat was a real hero. But she was, too!

Before Sophie could say anything, Toby Myers spoke up. "You don't know what you're talking about," he told Mindy.

Sophie's mouth dropped open. She could not believe it. Was Toby *standing up* for her?

Until the year before, this would not have surprised Sophie. Until the year before, she and Toby had been best friends. But things changed in second grade. Toby started hanging out with yucky Archie Dolan, and Kate moved to town. Now Sophie and Kate were best friends. And Sophie and Toby could not look at each other.

If they did, they had to stick out their tongues.

But maybe things were changing. . . .

Sophie thought of the day before, when Toby had actually done something *nice* for her. He had not made fun of her name that day—Sophie the Awesome—at all.

Was it possible? Could Toby be coming to his senses?

"*Real* heroes save the world from evil aliens and giant asteroids and killer robots!" Toby said. Then he looked at Sophie and stuck out his tongue.

No. Sophie sighed. She guessed he had not changed after all.

"Yeah!" said Archie. "And heroes have a mutant power." He pointed at Sophie with a sticky, stubby finger. "What's your mutant power, Sophie?" he asked.

Toby held his nose. "Super B.O.!" He laughed.

"Not funny," Kate said.

But Sophie rolled her eyes — and secretly sniffed her armpit, just to be sure.

No, she did not have B.O. And yes, no matter what Toby or Archie or Mindy said, Sophie was a hero.

She stuck her own tongue out at Toby.

So there!

CHAPTER 2

Sophie told her hero story so many times that day she was sure everyone had heard it. But she was ready to tell it again the next day as soon as she got to school. After all, it was such a great story! Or maybe she would let other people tell it. She liked that a lot, too.

The only thing was nobody seemed to want to hear her story anymore.

And there was something worse. No one seemed to want to call her Sophie the Hero, either.

Sophie did not understand it!

One day, she was a hero and everyone was

talking about her. The next day, they were talking about stuff like Dean's new haircut. And Eve's lost tooth. And Sophie A.'s fish, who just had babies. And Ben's mom, who just had her baby, too.

Okay. So maybe Dean's haircut was pretty funny-looking. And maybe a fish having babies was cool. But all kids lost their teeth. And all moms had babies. *At least one,* Sophie thought.

But not everyone was a hero!

How could they have forgotten about her already? Even after she'd drawn a big *H* for "hero" on her shirt with a marker that very morning.

Even Sophie's sidekick, Kate, was joking with Dean about his hair.

"You look like a giant toothbrush!" Kate said.

Oh, well, Sophie thought, trying to make herself feel better. Maybe they'd talk about her again once Dean's hair grew back.

She sure hoped so. She really, really liked being Sophie the Hero. And she really, really did not want to be Sophie the Nothing again.

Then the bell rang and their teacher, Ms. Moffly,

wrote two big words on the blackboard. As soon as Sophie read them, the day got brighter again.

LOCAL HEROES

Sophie could not believe it. Ms. Moffly was going to teach about *her*! And Sophie had not even told her hero story to the teacher yet. Wow! But of course Ms. Moffly had heard it. In fact, it was probably all they talked about in the teachers' lounge, Sophie bet.

"We have two very special guests today," Ms. Moffly said.

Hmm . . ., Sophie wondered. Who was number two? Ella? Mrs. Dixon? They weren't exactly heroes, like her. But they were part of the story.

"I hope you'll help me welcome them," Ms. Moffly went on.

Sophie took a deep breath and got ready to stand up.

"I'd like to introduce . . . Firefighters Burruss and Jones!" Ms. Moffly said.

Huh?

Sophie sat back and watched as two firefighters walked in.

One was a man. He was tall with lots of whiskers. He looked like Sophie's dad the time he'd almost grown a beard. The other was a woman. She was short and very pretty. Sophie thought that was good, since she was wearing the same blue shirt and pants and big black boots as the man.

"Hello, everyone," said the pretty firefighter.

"Hello," replied the class all together.

That is, everyone in the class but Sophie. She was so surprised she could not talk yet.

"Firefighters Burruss and Jones are here to teach us about fire safety," Ms. Moffly said. "Pay very close attention. It might save your life one day."

Sophie sighed. Of course, she knew that she was not the world's only hero.

She watched the firefighters take off their hats and set up some posters they had brought in. The pretty one smiled at Sophie, and Sophie sat up a little straighter so that the *H* on her shirt showed above her desk. She wondered if the firefighter guessed that Sophie was a hero, also.

Sophie knew that heroes had to respect each other. So she listened very carefully to all the things the firefighters said.

Things like "Don't hide; get outside," for when there was a fire in your house.

And "Stay low and go," since crawling along the ground was the best way to avoid smoke.

Sophie did not listen that hard when the firefighters told them what number to call in case of a fire or another big emergency. That was because she already knew it: 911. Of course.

But Sophie did listen to them tell how they got to be firefighters. She did not know they had to take tests and *then* go to firefighter school.

And she listened to them tell what they did at work—besides going grocery shopping in their uniforms and fire truck. (She had seen them at the Shop-Fresh more than once.)

Then came the moment Sophie had been waiting for: question time!

She quickly raised her hand as high as it would go. But if there was one thing Sophie was used to, it was being in the middle. In lines, and races, and question times, too. So she propped her arm up and waited as Toby asked a question first.

"What's the biggest fire you ever put out?" Toby asked.

The firefighters looked at each other.

"Probably that four-alarmer at the warehouse," the woman said. "We had to call in all three of our engines *and* three more from the next town."

"Sweet!" said Toby.

Next was Archie.

"Do you sweat a lot in those uniforms?" he asked. "And does it make them stink as bad as my brother's football pads?"

The pretty firefighter smiled. "Sometimes. Yes," she said.

Then Grace asked if the firchouse had a Dalmatian.

They did not. But they did have a lizard named Godzilla. It was a thank-you gift from a pet shop they had saved from burning down.

"Are you the same guys who saved my grandma when she got stuck in her old lawn chair?" Ben asked next. "That was so cool! They had to use the Jaws of Death!"

"I think you mean the Jaws of Life," said the tall firefighter, grinning. "And sorry, no. It wasn't us."

"Have you ever rescued a kitten from a tree?" was Mia's question.

"No, we haven't," said the pretty firefighter. "But we did rescue a puppy from a well in the spring."

Then, at last—finally!—the tall firefighter pointed to Sophie.

Sophie rubbed her tired arm, then smoothed her shirt. And she cleared her throat proudly.

"I just wanted to know...," she began, "have you ever stopped a little kindergartner from running into the street to catch her runaway

Slinkys and saved her from probably being squashed by a car? And wouldn't you call someone who did that a big hero?"

The pretty firefighter shook her head. "No, I have not," she said. "And yes! That is very heroic. Isn't it, Jim?"

Sophie felt her cheeks and ears—and even her insides—get warm and pinkish.

The firefighter with whiskers nodded. "Sure is," he said. "And it brings up a good point, too. Never run into the street. Not for anything. Ever."

Then there was a little cough, and Mindy raised her hand. Her face always looked pinchy to Sophie, but it looked extra-pinchy then.

"I have a question in two parts," Mindy said.

"Okay," said the firefighter with whiskers. "Go ahead."

"One," Mindy began, "have you ever rescued five kittens from a burning building like Scarlett the cat? And two: Do you agree that she is one of the biggest heroes ever?"

The firefighters shook their heads. "No, we haven't." Then they nodded. "And yes . . . she sure is."

Mindy turned to Sophie. She looked extra, super sassy. But Sophie crossed her arms and raised her chin and looked right back.

Meanwhile, Ms. Moffly stood up and shook the firefighters' hands.

"This has been a wonderful visit," she told them. "We can't thank you enough. But I know you have to get back to the firehouse. And we have to get to gym." She looked around the room. "Class, please thank Firefighters Burruss and Jones for coming, won't you? And thank them for being our heroes every day."

The firefighters waved.

"Bye! Thank you!" the class said.

"Yes! Thank you!" Sophie yelled.

In fact, she yelled so loud even Toby stared.

But Sophie did not care. About Toby. Or Mindy. Or anything. The firefighters had spoken. She felt like Sophie the Hero again!

But Sophie realized something else. If she was going to stay a hero, she needed to be like the firefighters. She needed to be a hero every day.

And I will! thought Sophie.

Let the hero work begin!

CHAPTER 3

Sophie was on the lookout all the way to gym. She did not want to miss any chance to be a hero.

"Tell me if you see anyone who needs saving," she whispered to Kate.

"Okay," said Kate. She looked down the line of kids following Ms. Moffly. "Uh... saving how?" she whispered back.

Sophie shrugged. She did not know. She really wished there were a busy street to cross. Or a den full of thieves to pass. Why did schools have to be so safe? Especially the gym! There wasn't a thing to trip over, and all the walls were padded.

As they entered the gym, Kate grabbed Sophie's arm. "Save me!" she panted.

"What? What is it?" asked Sophie, excited.

Kate leaned her head back and rolled her eyes up. "From this smell!" she said. Then she lifted her head and grinned. "Get it?" She held her nose. "This place smells like moldy meatballs!"

Sophie always thought the gym smelled more like sour sweat socks. But she basically agreed. Still, she tried not to laugh. Being a hero was serious business!

Once they all sat down on the bleachers, the gym teacher, Mr. Hurley, made an announcement.

"Today we're going outside!" he hollered. (Hollering was how he talked.)

Sophie pumped her fist. Hooray!

After all, anything could happen outside! There could be a tornado. Or a wildfire. Or a tiger escaped from the zoo!

Who cared if there was no zoo in Sophie's town? Or anywhere close? The farther a tiger had to come, the better. Then they would have to write about it in the newspaper. And that was always good for a hero!

Once they were outside, Mr. Hurley split the class into two teams. Today they were playing kickball, and today that was just fine with Sophie.

Usually, Sophie did not like kickball much. Mostly because she played the same middle position — center field — every time. And that made it a very boring game for Sophie. The ball always seemed to go to the left or the right.

But today that would give Sophie lots of time to be on the lookout for people who needed saving!

Sophie waved to Kate, who was on the other team. Then she took her place and scanned the field for danger.

Sniff, sniff. She sniffed the air for smoke. Or a wild tiger.

She searched the sky for aliens. Or asteroids.

Sophie was ready for any danger she could think of.

Of course, Sophie knew she could not stop a wildfire. Or a tiger. Or an alien. Or an asteroid. But she could be the first to tell everyone to run!

"Sophie, pay attention!" she heard Mr. Hurley holler.

Huh?

Sophie turned. She was stunned, but not because Mr. Hurley was hollering and waving his arms. He always did that. She was stunned that someone had kicked the ball to center field... and that it was rolling right past her!

Sophie ran after the ball.

"Aw, Sophie! Hurry! You should have had that!" her teammates cried.

"Yay, Kate!" she heard the other team cheer as Kate scored a home run.

Sophie finally stopped the ball and rolled it back to the pitcher. She really wished that Toby hadn't been the pitcher right then. He was frowning at her. Hard.

"I bet you did that on purpose, to help Kate!" he yelled.

Sophie stuck out her tongue at Toby. "Of course I didn't!" she told him.

Sure, Sophie was happy for Kate. But she would never try to make her team lose.

She put her hands on her hips and told herself to pay attention. It was not going to be easy to be a hero *and* play kickball. But she would have to try.

Sophie kept her eyes on the field. And the ball. And the players. And before she knew it, she got her chance to be a hero—by saving Grace!

Grace was in right field. Someone had kicked the ball to her and it was sailing right toward her head.

Sophie knew she had to hurry. She ran across the field at top speed. And she gave Grace a giant push.

They both fell—*thud!* The ball flew past them and rolled away.

Grace jumped up and glared at Sophie. "I could have caught that!" she said.

"Are you kidding? That ball was headed straight for your head!" Sophie said.

Then Sophie heard the words that filled her with tingles. It was Mr. Hurley hollering, "Good job, Sophie! Way to go!"

"See?" she said to Grace. Even Mr. Hurley could see she was a hero!

Then she realized something. Mr. Hurley was hollering to Sophie A., not her.

Sophie A. had kicked the ball...and scored another run.

"Sorry, Grace," Sophie mumbled as she trudged back to center field.

"What does that big 'H' on your shirt stand for, anyway? *Horrible?*" Toby groaned from the pitcher's mound.

Grrr! Sophie glared. She was too mad to stick her tongue out. "No, it's for 'hero,'" she said under her breath.

Sophie would show him. She had to save someone *soon!*

But she was also kind of ready for the inning to end.

Then suddenly her eyes popped wide open. There was something buzzing around second base — and Dean's head — right in front of her!

What if it was a bee?

What if Dean was allergic?

What if it stung him and he swelled up like Sophie's cousin Will did once? Sophie's Aunt Jan had called the ambulance and everything!

But even if Dean was not allergic, nobody liked to get stung. One time a bee stung the bottom of Sophie's foot and she couldn't walk on it for a week.

Sophie had to get rid of that bee so she could be Dean's hero!

For one second, Sophie worried that the bee might sting her. But she knew that was not how a hero's mind worked. So she ran up to Dean and started whacking.

She meant to whack the bee, of course. But Dean's head got in the way.

"Ow! Stop! Help! My hair! What are you doing?" Dean cried.

"It's a bee! It's a bee!" yelled Sophie. "Oh, wait..." She looked at the bug more closely. "Never mind. It's just a fly."

Then she saw Dean's hair. It still looked like a toothbrush, but now it looked like a toothbrush that a dog had chewed on. Sophie tried not to laugh...but everyone else did.

"Back to your positions!" Mr. Hurley hollered.

"Uh, sorry, Dean," Sophie said. She was careful not to look at him. And then, at last, it was their team's turn to kick.

Sophie, of course, was in the middle of the lineup. But for once, she didn't mind. It gave her time to look out for more danger.

Soon the bases were loaded and Toby was up. Sydney was on third base and ready to run.

Then Sophie noticed something. Sydney's sneaker was untied. She could trip and break her leg! It was Sophie the Hero time!

Sophie dashed out of the dugout as Kate pitched the ball to Toby. She bent down and grabbed Sydney's shoe just as Toby kicked the ball. Then she started to tie Sydney's laces as Sydney began to run.

The next thing Sophie knew, Sydney was falling down—on top of her. Then came the runners from second—*oof!*—and first—*ugh!*

Sophie crawled out of the pile just as Archie tagged them all out.

Then Mr. Hurley blew his whistle. "Game over!" he hollered.

CHAPTER 4

Sophie wasn't feeling much like a hero after gym.

Art class came next. She wasn't sure how to be a hero there, exactly. But a true hero could be a hero anywhere, she guessed.

She also had a papier-mâché animal to finish. The class had molded them the week before. Now it was time to paint them.

"What color would you like, Sophie?" Ms. Bart, the art teacher, asked her.

Sophie really liked Ms. Bart. She probably liked her best of all her teachers. (And not just because Ms. Bart still had Sophie's picture of a snow princess from the year before hanging in her classroom.)

Sophie also liked Ms. Bart because she was fun to look at. She was short and had long, long hair. She always wore it in a braid that went way past her bottom. And it was splattered with paint. Just like her clothes. And shoes. And skin.

The year before, Sophie had learned about camouflage. That was what Ms. Bart always made her think of. Sophie wondered: If Ms. Bart stood very still in her art room, would she blend in?

Sophie smiled at Ms. Bart. "I'll take red, please," Sophie told her.

"Red, huh? Okay!" Ms. Bart smiled at her. "Not the usual color for an alligator. But I like the way you think!"

Sophie looked down at her papier-mâché animal. "It's a fox," she said.

Ms. Bart handed her the red paint. "Oh... so it is!" she said.

Next Kate took some gray paint.

36

"Is that a mouse?" the teacher asked her.

Kate held it up. "It was," she said. "But I don't know." She touched its extra-pointy nose. "I think I'm going to make it the world's smallest elephant, instead."

Ms. Bart laughed and moved down the table, giving out more paint. Then she stopped next to Archie and Toby. They were snarling and growling while their papier-mâché creatures battled.

Archie raised his animal and banged it down on Toby's animal's head. "T. rex always beats crocodile," he said.

"T. rex?" Ms. Bart repeated. "Oh, Archie. I can't believe it! I thought I told you to make something else, just this once. You've drawn and painted and sculpted nothing but dinosaurs for three years."

Archie shrugged. "It could be a dog, I guess," he said.

"Never mind," Ms. Bart said. "If dinosaurs inspire you, it's fine, I suppose. Okay, class. Paint away!" she announced.

Mindy raised her hand.

"Excuse me, Ms. Bart," she said, "but I'm not happy with this blue you gave me."

"Oh, no?" said the art teacher.

"No," Mindy said. She held up the cup of paint and wrinkled her nose as if it smelled bad. "This is much too ordinary. I need something more brilliant for my peacock."

"Me too!" Lily added.

Ms. Bart looked surprised. So did the rest of the class. They weren't surprised that Lily copied Mindy. She always did that. But each of them was supposed to make an animal that was different from anyone else's. Everyone knew that. It was the only rule Ms. Bart had given them . . . mostly because of Lily.

"Did you make a peacock, too?" Kate asked Lily.

"Uh . . ." Lily bit her lip. "No . . . I mean, not really."

Ms. Bart walked up beside her. "Do you mean you made a pea*hen*? A female? Instead of a male peacock?" she asked.

Lily nodded quickly.

"Wonderful!" said Ms. Bart. "Then let me get you some brown paint. That's usually the color of a peahen. And they don't have that same fancy tail, so maybe we should get rid of that?"

Lily slumped in her seat. "Fine," she said.

Sophie tried not to giggle.

Ms. Bart dragged a stool to a wall of shelves across the art room. Then she began to climb.

"I'm pretty sure I have the perfect blue up here somewhere," she said.

She reached for the top shelf and picked through some jars and boxes.

"Ooh! Steady!" she suddenly cried.

That was when Sophie looked up and saw the stool wobble. Not a lot. But enough.

Uh-oh!

Ms. Bart could fall...unless Sophie the Hero saved her!

Sophie handed her paintbrush to Kate. "Hold this!" she told her sidekick.

"Huh?" said Kate.

Then Sophie jumped up, ran across the room, and grabbed Ms. Bart's ankles.

"Don't worry, Ms. Bart, I've got you! You're safe!" she said.

"Oh, Sophie, no!" Ms. Bart cried, grabbing the paint shelf. "Look out!"

☆ ☆ ☆

The good news was: All the paint on the shelf did not fall on the art teacher.

The bad news was: It fell on Sophie. Every drop.

Sophie was covered with paint from head to toe. And she did not feel like a hero. She felt like a papier-mâché blob.

Still, she was not as upset as Mindy.

"That blue paint was perfect!" Mindy wailed. "And now it's all gone!"

Sophie was very happy that Ms. Bart let her go clean up in the bathroom. And that she let Kate, Sophie's sidekick, go, too. Mindy's whining hurt her paint-covered ears a lot.

"Hey, cheer up," Kate told Sophie in the bathroom. "You might have really saved Ms. Bart. Who knows?"

"Yeah," Sophie said, sighing. But she was not sure Ms. Bart thought so.

"And on the bright side," Kate went on, "now you look more like a hero!"

"I do?" Sophie asked.

"Yeah!" Kate nodded. "Totally—Peacock Girl!"

Sophie rolled her eyes. Then she opened the zip-top bag that held her set of Emergency Clothes.

Sophie always thought Emergency Clothes were for kids who couldn't make it to the bathroom. (Like her. In kindergarten. When she drank three milks at lunch.) And since she had learned her lesson (one milk at the most!), she thought she would never need them.

No such luck.

Sophie guessed that her Emergency Clothes were better than a paint-covered shirt and skirt. But not much. The pants were too short. And the shirt was the one that Sophie hated most. The pink one that said "Kiss me, I'm a princess!"

Yuck!

Kate looked at her. "Ooh! You could call yourself—" she began.

But Sophie held up her hand. "Don't even say it."

She could not wait to get home and change and start being a hero again!

CHAPTER 5

When she and Kate finally got to Sophie's house, Sophie closed the door behind them with a sigh.

Phew! It was great to be Ella's hero, but two days of it was enough. Sophie hoped the next person she saved did not hang on her so much.

"Why didn't you let Ella come in?" Kate asked her. "She's so cute. And she carried your backpack all the way home."

"Because I'm sore from Ella hugging me," Sophie said, rubbing her sides. "And because we need to talk about important hero stuff."

Sophie dropped her backpack on the floor. Then she froze as the door opened again.

Oh, no. Not Ella!

But it was just Sophie's big sister, Hayley, and her best friend, Kim. They were giggling about something—probably boys. As usual.

All of a sudden—*BANG!*—there was a loud sound from the kitchen.

Sophie and Hayley looked at each other. They both knew what had made the noise: Max, their little brother.

For a long time, Max had been their baby brother. But now that he was two, he was not a baby anymore. Now he could run. And climb. And kick. And almost jump.

And he did. All the time.

There was one thing Max did not do, though. And that was talk.

Sophie thought this was a big problem. All the other two-year-olds she saw could talk. And talk. And talk. But Sophie's parents said that

Max would talk when he was ready. Sophie was not sure about that. But she hoped so.

In the meantime, Max made a lot of other noises.

BANG! BANG! BANG!

Then Sophie heard another noise.

Meow, meow, meow!

A gray ball of fur dashed toward them. Sophie bent down and scooped it up.

"It's okay, Tiptoe. I've got you," Sophie said. She gently rubbed it with her nose.

Tiptoe was Sophie's brand-new kitten. She and Hayley had picked her out at a shelter two weeks before.

There had been so many kittens, Sophie had thought it would be hard to pick just one. But Tiptoe was hanging on the door of her cage by her tiny claws. Sophie knew right away that the kitten wanted them to take her home.

Of course, the kitten did not know there was a *Max* waiting at home.

Poor Tiptoe.

Sophie cuddled her tightly. Then she went into the kitchen with Hayley, Kim, and Kate.

Every cabinet was open. The floor was covered with pots and pans.

That was how the kitchen always looked when Max was there.

"Hi, girls," said Sophie's mom. She was pulling Max down from the counter. "Okay, Max. Game over. Time to put everything away," she said.

Max shook his head and grabbed a spoon.

Then he looked at Sophie and started to laugh.

"Sophie!" her mom gasped. She was not laughing. "What happened to you? Your hair is all blue!"

Sophie shrugged. "Just trying to be a hero," she said.

Hayley rolled her eyes at Kim. "Third graders," she groaned.

"What happened?" Sophie's mom asked again. "I see you had to change clothes. Oh, I love that shirt so much!"

Sophie sighed, but she did not feel like

explaining. Especially not with Hayley and Kim there, too.

Hayley was not a bad sister. In fact, she was great . . . when it was just the two of them. But she was not always that great when she was with her fifth-grade friends. With them, she acted like she was grown-up and super-cool.

Too cool for Sophie.

"So?" Sophie's mom said.

Sophie had to change the subject. She pointed at her brother. "Look out," she said. "Max is going for the cat food."

Sophie's mother chased after Max, while Hayley grabbed the last two apples out of the fruit bowl. She took a bite of one and handed the other to Kim.

Sophie sighed. The apples were the green kind, her favorite. She would have liked one just then.

"Hey, guess what, Mom," Hayley said. She took another juicy bite and chewed it. "Mr. Bloom brought in a pet for our classroom. Guess what it is!"

"A hamster?" asked Kate. Sophie knew she loved those. She had five . . . no, six . . . no, eight?

"No." Hayley shook her head. "A snake. A *corn* snake, actually. And guess what we named him?" She shared a smile with Kim. "You never will."

"Rumplesnakeskin," Sophie said.

Hayley stared at her. "How did you know?"

Sophie shared her own smile with Kate. "Just smart, I guess."

(That and she had heard Hayley talking about it on the bus home.)

Their mom came back with Max. "How wonderful!" she said. She got a big smile on her face. "You know, I used to love catching snakes when I was your age."

Kate's eyes got big. But Sophie was not surprised at all. Her dad hated creepy-crawly things, but Sophie's mom did not mind them. Spiders. Crickets. Bats. If any critter ever snuck into the house, she was always the one who caught it.

Sophie thought that must be why she was so good at catching Max.

"I hope you got to hold the snake. Did you?" Sophie's mom asked Hayley.

Hayley and Kim nodded.

"Was it gross?" Kate asked.

"No," said Hayley. "It was great. Rumplesnakeskin's not gross at all, or slimy. He's soft and smooth. But snakes can still have germs. So you have to wash your hands after you touch one."

Washing hands. *Humph.* That did not sound great to Sophie.

"And I bet you guys didn't know this!" Hayley went on. She looked down at Kate and Sophie. "Snakes smell with their tongues, not their noses. And they sleep with their eyes open."

"Why?" Kate asked. "Are they afraid your mom is going to catch them?"

Sophie's mom laughed, but Hayley shook her head.

"Because they don't have eyelids, of course," she told Kate matter-of-factly.

"Really? No eyelids? That's weird!" Kate said.

Sophie had had enough of Hayley's snake lesson.

Plus she knew that any second now, Max would get down and start banging things again.

She grabbed two bananas from the fruit bowl. They were too green for Hayley, but that was just how Sophie liked them.

"Come on, Kate. Let me change my shirt. Then we can go out to the playhouse," she said.

"Hang on!" Sophie's mom said. "Don't you want to take a shower?" She lunged for Max as he pulled open the fridge. "Not so fast, young man!"

Sophie felt her pigtails. They were stiff and crunchy, and she knew they were bright blue. But now that the paint was dry, it didn't feel that bad.

"Nah. I'll take one later," she said.

Sophie had wasted too much time already. She still had to make a heroic plan!

She pulled Kate toward the stairs. "Yell if you need a hero!" she called back over her shoulder.

☆   ☆   ☆

As soon as she had changed, Sophie led Kate outside to her playhouse. She had the bananas in her pocket and Tiptoe in her hands.

Sophie's playhouse had been Hayley's, until she got too big for it. Now Sophie was getting too big, too. She had to duck when she went in. But there was still just enough room for two third graders inside. And it was still Sophie's favorite place to have long, important talks with her best friend.

It used to be Sophie's favorite place to play Hansel and Gretel with Toby. But that was back when they had been little. Back when *they* had been best friends.

Sophie sat down on a small wooden chair and let Tiptoe tiptoe around her feet. Then she reached for the pencil and notepad on the counter.

"Okay," she said, trying to be businesslike. "What are some other things I can do to be a hero?"

"Hmm..." Kate thought for a second. Then she leaned out the little playhouse window. "Ooh, check out that giant spiderweb!"

Sophie watched her friend. "Hey! That's it!" she said.

"What?" Kate said.

"You pretend to fall out the classroom window tomorrow, and I'll catch you!" Sophie said.

Kate looked at her funny. "I don't think so," she said.

"Why not?" Sophie asked. "I promise I'll catch you. And even if I don't...we're on the first floor."

Kate crossed her arms and looked at Sophie the way her mom sometimes did.

"Okay. Fine," Sophie said. She knew it wasn't the best idea. But it was something.

"Besides, I'm your *sidekick*," Kate said. "I need to be *beside* you, not hanging out the window."

"You're right," Sophie said, scratching her crunchy, paint-covered head. She drew a big curly question mark on her paper. "But my next heroic deed has to be something good, like the firefighters talked about this morning."

Kate nodded. "Right," she said. "Like the school catching fire so you can save everyone or something."

Sophie's felt her eyebrows jump up. "Exactly!" she said.

"But we don't want the school to catch fire," Kate said quickly.

"No. Of course not." Sophie shook her head. "But what if I pull the fire alarm anyway? What if I tell everyone I *thought* there was a fire? And that I was *trying* to save them?"

She could almost hear the cheers. She could imagine Principal Tate giving her a great big medal!

Then she saw Kate shake her head.

"If you pull the alarm, ink will spray out. And you'll get kicked out of school," Kate said.

"Oh . . . too bad," Sophie said. She sighed.

She put down her notepad and picked up Tiptoe.

Would she ever think of some way to be a hero again?

What were other hero things firefighters did? If only she had some Jaws of Life! Or was it Jaws of Death? (And what were they, exactly?)

"Ouch!" Sophie cried all of a sudden. Tiptoe had grabbed her hair.

She reached up and gently pried the kitten's claws loose. The dried paint made it harder. Then a thought hit Sophie smack in the middle of her blue head.

"Come on, Kate! It's time to rescue a kitten from a tree!" she said.

They ran outside, and Sophie tried her best to get Tiptoe to climb the pine tree.

Then the maple tree.

Then the elm tree.

But Tiptoe did not want to climb any tree at all.

In fact, the more Sophie tried to help her, the more tightly Tiptoe clung to Sophie. Sophie was glad the kitten's claws were so tiny. Or they might have hurt. A lot.

Oh, well. Sophie sighed. She set Tiptoe down on the grass beside her. Then she pulled the bananas out of her pocket and handed one to Kate.

Sophie peeled hers with a frown and gloomily

took a bite. Then she chewed it, thinking hard. And slowly, she began to smile.

Sophie pulled the peel all the way off her banana. Then she held it up in front of Kate's face.

"I've got it!" Sophie declared. "This is just what I need to be a hero!"

CHAPTER 6

The next day, in the lunch line, Sophie took a banana. It had some brown spots. But for once, that was okay.

Sophie and Kate sat down, but not at their usual table. They sat at the one by the trash can, near the tray rack.

Sophie quickly ate her banana. It tasted better than it looked. At the same time, Kate dug into her food. It was her favorite: breakfast for lunch.

"Are you really going to do it?" Kate asked. She slurped some syrup off her spoon.

Sophie nodded. When the coast was clear, she tossed her banana peel onto the floor.

Then Sophie stuck a finger into her syrup and licked it. But she was too excited to eat more. Besides, she liked pancakes with chocolate chips. But plain? Not so much.

Sophie sat back and waited. She had everything planned out. All the students had to walk by her to put away their trays. She just needed someone to slip on the banana peel. Then Sophie would jump up and save the person. She would be a hero again! (And she'd drawn an *H* on another shirt to be ready.)

It was hard for Sophie to wait for everyone to finish eating. But at last, some kids got up to clear their trays.

Sophie moved to the edge of her seat. "This is it!" she whispered to Kate.

Except it was not. Because nobody slipped.

Sophie stared hard at the floor, and even harder at the banana peel. At least a hundred feet stepped over it—but not one touched it.

"I can't believe it!" Sophie told Kate.

"I know," Kate said. "Hey, are you going to eat that?" She pointed to Sophie's pancakes.

Sophie slid them over. "Go ahead."

"Thanks! We sidekicks have to keep up our strength," Kate said, digging in.

Of course, Sophie was glad that some people did not slip. Like Dean, since he was the biggest kid in her class. Could Sophie really catch him if he fell?

She wasn't sure about that.

And then there was Mindy, who walked by with Lily. They were pointing and giggling and Mindy's foot *almost* touched the peel.

Phew! Sophie was glad it missed! She knew she could save Mindy, but she did not really want to. That would be as bad as saving Archie or Toby, who walked by next.

Sophie held her breath and kept her eyes down. She watched their sneakers step up to the peel... and stop.

"Check it out," said Archie. "There's a banana peel on the floor!"

Sophie felt Kate kick her under the table. Her throat got very tight, and her heart beat a little faster. Was Archie going to pick it up and ruin her plan?

But Archie had something different in mind. "Geronimooo!" he yelled as he jumped and landed—*SPLAT!*—right on the banana peel.

To Sophie's surprise, he did not slip. He just jumped off.

"Sweet!" Toby yelled.

The boys high-fived and walked away.

"Aw. Too bad," said Kate.

The peel looked darker and flatter. But more slippery, too, Sophie thought.

"No, it's okay," Sophie told Kate. "The next person that steps on it will slip for sure!"

The only thing was almost every kid in third grade—except Sophie and Kate—had already put his or her tray away.

Ms. Moffly was walking around the cafeteria. "Time to go, class," she called.

Kate licked the last drop of syrup off her plate and stood up. "Come on, Sophie," she said. "Recess time. We've got to go."

"I know," Sophie said slowly. And she sighed — half because she had eaten a brown banana for nothing, and half because she had not gotten a chance to be a hero.

Then, suddenly, Sophie saw something that made her grab Kate's shoulder. Ms. Moffly was headed straight for the banana peel!

"Uh-oh," said Kate under her breath.

But Sophie shook her head quickly. Kate did not understand. There was a very clear picture in Sophie's mind — a picture of her saving Ms. Moffly. If she did that, she would be the biggest hero in the world!

Sophie stood up and pushed in her chair. She was ready to spring into action!

But Ms. Moffly did not slip. Instead, she stopped, bent down, and picked up the peel. The teacher shook her head and tossed the banana peel into the trash can. Then she turned and smiled at Kate and Sophie.

"That was close. I might have slipped!" she said. "Now hurry and clean up, girls. It's time for recess."

"That *was* close!" Kate said as they watched Ms. Moffly walk off.

"I know," Sophie groaned. "If only she *had* slipped. That would have been awesome!"

Kate looked at her. "What do you mean?"

"I mean, I could have saved Ms. Moffly!" Sophie said. "Then I would have been *her* hero!"

Sophie sighed as she picked up her tray and walked over to the trash can. "Oh, if only she had sli—*AGH!*"

And that was when Sophie stepped right on the slippery spot where the banana peel had been. Her feet flew up. Her tray flew back. And she landed—*OUCH!*—smack on her bottom.

Kate ran to her side. "Are you okay, Sophie?" she asked.

Sophie looked down at the syrupy plate stuck to the front of her shirt. The big *H* was completely covered.

"I guess. But I might need to use your set of Emergency Clothes today," Sophie told Kate glumly.

Then Sophie looked up to see the fifth graders coming in. It was time for their lunch. Sophie's sister, Hayley, was walking next to Kim.

"Hey, Hayley," said another girl. "Isn't that your sister?"

Sophie quickly closed her eyes. She did not want to see Hayley laugh. Or roll her eyes. Or shake her head.

But then she felt a hand on her arm. "What happened?" Hayley asked.

Sophie shrugged. "Just trying to be a hero. That, and the floor's a little slippery, I guess."

Hayley almost rolled her eyes then. But instead, she helped Sophie up. "*Try* to be more careful," she said.

"I will," said Sophie.

Kate patted Sophie's shoulder. "I'll make sure she does," Kate said. Then she added, "Hey, how's Rumplesnakeskin?"

Hayley smiled. "Oh, he's good. But he sure freaked out our student teacher today," she said with a laugh. Then Hayley gave a little wave, flipped her hair, and went back to her friends.

That was when Sophie smiled the biggest smile she'd smiled all day. Not just because she really loved Hayley. But also because her sister had given her a super-amazing, totally heroic idea!

CHAPTER 7

Sophie and Kate headed outside for recess, but Sophie did not plan to stay for long. She had a different plan: to sneak inside her sister's classroom while the fifth grade was at lunch. She'd find their snake and borrow it to take back to her own classroom.

Then the fun part would start!

Sophie would hide the snake somewhere Ms. Moffly would surely find it. And when Ms. Moffly did find it—and freaked out!—Sophie would run up, grab Rumplesnakeskin, and save the day. Then she would be Ms. Moffly's hero!

It was simple!

All Sophie had to do was tell the yard monitor that she had to go inside to use the bathroom. And she *would* go to the bathroom eventually (to wash her hands when she was done moving Rumple-snakeskin).

"Okay, I'm ready! Let's go," said Kate.

But Sophie shook her head.

"You know only one girl can go to the bathroom at a time," she told Kate. "If we both go, then people will know that something is up."

Kate nodded."But what if I *really* have to go to the bathroom?" she asked. "Then what?"

Sophie bit her lip. That was a good question. "I guess you'll have to hold it," she said.

"I'll *try*," Kate groaned, trying not to smile.

"Thanks." Sophie knew she was very lucky to have such a good sidekick. "Okay, wish me luck," she went on. "I'm going in."

Sophie got the bathroom pass from the yard monitor. Then she went back into school and hurried toward the bathroom... but she did not go in.

Instead, she turned right and went up the stairs to Hayley's classroom.

Sophie slipped inside the room and sighed two big sighs. One sigh was because she had just run up three flights of stairs. The other was because no one had stopped her. Yay!

Then Sophie looked around. *Wow. Poor Hayley,* she thought. Hayley always made fifth grade sound so cool. But it did not look half as much fun as third. For one thing, there were no games. Not anywhere. Not one. And no reading corner with a cozy rug. There were no self-portraits of each student. And no chart to tell you what special job you got to do that week.

All Sophie saw were desks and chairs and maps and charts and boring posters with tons of words. And lots and lots of cursive writing all over the board. Plus thick books that looked like they had four pictures inside—at the most.

Still, Sophie had an urge to sit at Hayley's desk, just to see what it felt like to be her. But there were no name tags on the chairs to tell Sophie which one was her sister's.

Oh, well. That was okay. Sophie did not have time to sit. She had to find Rumplesnakeskin.

It was not hard to find his tank at the back of the room. It was big and had a sign on the bottom with his name. But it was hard to find Rumplesnakeskin!

All Sophie could see inside the tank were shredded newspapers, a shoe box, and a bowl of water. She could not believe it! Had someone stolen the fifth graders' snake before she could?

But then she saw something orange poking out from the shoe box.

"Aha!" she said out loud. "There you are!"

She lifted the top of the tank and carefully picked up the shoe box. Underneath was the snake!

Wow! He's so pretty! Sophie thought. Rumplesnakeskin was bright orange and white and yellow. And he was all twisted up. He looked like a candy-corn rope. Almost.

The snake's eyes were open . . . but he was not moving.

Maybe he was napping. Hooray! That was fine with Sophie. If the snake was sleeping, this would be even easier than she'd hoped!

Sophie had never touched a snake before. She was a little nervous. But if her mom and Hayley could do it, so could she. It was in her blood!

Sophie reached in and picked up Rumplesnakeskin. Hayley was right—snakes were not slimy. They were dry and smooth and scaly.

Sophie held him up to get a closer look. Suddenly, his tongue flicked out.

"Ah!" Sophie yelped. She couldn't help it. His body began to move and twist and wrap around her arm.

Sophie looked down at her new thick orange bracelet. Boy! The snake liked her—a lot!

Rumplesnakeskin reached his head out. Then he flicked his tongue toward her shirt.

Sophie looked down at the spot near her *H*. "That's syrup," she told him.

Unfortunately, Sophie did not have time to stand around chatting with Rumplesnakeskin. She had to get back to room 10 and hide him before recess was over.

But it was one thing for someone to see her running around the halls during recess. It was another thing for someone to see her running around the halls during recess with the fifth graders' snake.

What if somebody stopped her?

It was not easy to hide a bright orange snake. Especially when he was on your arm (and slowly making his way to your shoulder).

Somehow, she had to hide him.

Sophie looked around the room quickly and spotted Hayley's pink jean jacket on a hook. It was Hayley's favorite. She would be *so* mad if Sophie stole it. But Sophie was not stealing. She was borrowing. And she would make sure Hayley got it back.

And then she could be *Hayley's* hero!

Sophie smiled as she draped the jacket over her shoulder to cover the snake. Then she hurried into the hall and down the stairs to room 10.

She was almost there when she heard someone say, "Sophie Miller?"

Uh-oh.

Sophie stopped and turned around. Ms. Bart, the art teacher, was walking up behind her. She had a lunch box in her hand. (It was covered with paint. Of course.)

Sophie quickly checked Hayley's jacket. It was doing its job. Good.

Then she froze. What was Rumplesnakeskin doing? Was he moving up her arm?

No! No! Not to her underarm! Sophie was ticklish there! But the snake did not care.

"I thought that was you," Ms. Bart went on as Sophie squirmed. "I'm glad all that paint came out of your hair. Believe me, I know how hard it is to wash out."

Sophie wanted to say, "I'm glad, too." But she could not.

Instead, she laughed.

And laughed.

And laughed.

The snake was tickling her worse than her mom or dad or cousin Will ever had!

"I'm glad you can laugh about it," Ms. Bart said. "That's how I am, too."

Sophie laughed.

And laughed.

And laughed some more.

"Okay, well . . . ," Ms. Bart said. She looked at Sophie a little funny. "I'm going to go eat my lunch now."

Sophie nodded. She was still laughing and trying to catch her breath. She ducked into her classroom as fast as she could.

Phew! That was a close one. But Sophie did not think about that too much. All she could think about was getting Rumplesnakeskin out of her armpit!

She gently took him into her other hand. Now she had to hide him somewhere in the classroom, fast! Recess would be over soon.

Sophie looked around. Then she saw just the place. Ms. Moffly's desk. *Bingo!*

She walked up and opened a drawer. But when she tried to put Rumplesnakeskin inside, he did not want to go.

"You're as bad as Tiptoe," Sophie told him as he slid back up her arm. "But it's okay. I'll get you out soon, I promise. Look, there's a box of tissues in there. It will be almost like home."

Finally, the snake turned to the drawer and flicked his tongue. Sophie hoped the drawer smelled good to him. She guessed it did when he slid in and curled up next to Ms. Moffly's hairbrush.

"Good snake!" Sophie said.

Sophie squeezed her hands together. She felt a tingle. This was such a good plan! She was going to be a hero—a big one—again very soon!

Then Sophie looked down at her hands. Oh, yeah. She'd better wash those.

Sophie said good-bye—for now—to Rumple-snakeskin and ran to the bathroom.

She stood by the sink. And she looked in the mirror. Her smile was big. But she made it even bigger.

Perfect!

That was just the smile Sophie would use when Ms. Moffly called her "My hero!"

CHAPTER 8

Sophie made it back to the yard just before the end of recess.

"Mission accomplished!" she told Kate.

"Awesome!" Kate said, giving her a very heroic high five.

When the bell rang, the class followed Ms. Moffly back to room 10. But Sophie was so excited she kept walking too fast, making the line bend.

"Hey, Sophie," Ben said, "do you mind? *I'm* the Line Leader this week. Not you."

Sophie sighed and let Ben go ahead. But she did mind. A little bit.

What if Ms. Moffly found Rumplesnakeskin before Sophie got into the classroom? What if she suddenly wanted to fix her hair and ran to her desk to get her brush? Or what if a fly flew up her nose and she had to get a tissue?

A hero had to be there. Right then!

Luckily, Ms. Moffly did not open her drawer before Sophie got there.

But she did not open it after Sophie got there, either. Ms. Moffly sat down in her chair in the reading corner instead.

It was Chapter Book Time. *Ugh!*

For maybe the first time ever, Sophie did not want it to be Chapter Book Time. She plopped down on the reading rug with a frown.

"What's wrong?" Kate whispered. "Everything's going just like you planned."

Sophie pointed to Ms. Moffly's desk. "Ms. Moffly can't open her drawer from across the room," she whispered back.

Kate nodded. "Oh, right. But she'll open it later. Don't worry," she said. "I can't wait to hear how she screams. Can you?" she added. "Ooh, I hope she faints! Then I can fan her while you grab the snake!"

Ms. Moffly clapped her hands three times. "Quiet, everyone. Let's begin," she said, opening the book. "Oh! I forgot my glasses. Toby, would you please get them from my desk?"

From her desk?

Sophie looked at Kate. And Kate looked at Sophie.

What if *Toby* found the snake? Sophie had not thought of that!

She could still be a hero. She could save Toby instead of Ms. Moffly. But it would not be the same. Not at all!

Sophie held her breath. She watched Toby walk to the desk and reach for the drawer handle.

"No, no, Toby," Ms. Moffly said. "My glasses are right there, on top. Thank you."

Sophie sighed as Toby grabbed them and walked back to the reading rug. Another close call!

Ms. Moffly put her glasses on and opened the book again.

That week's book was about a mouse and a motorcycle. But the mouse had just lost the motorcycle. Sophie was not sure what would happen next. The day before, Sophie had really wanted to find out. But today, not so much. She had other things on her mind.

Things like Archie's sneezing. And green stuff coming out. And Ms. Moffly telling him to get a tissue from her desk.

Sophie bit her lip. Would *Archie* find the snake now?

Nope. He used his sleeve instead of getting a tissue. "That's okay, Ms. Moffly," he said.

Then Sydney had to go to the bathroom. She went to Ms. Moffly's desk to get the hall pass.

Then Eve found a tack in her shoe. She went to Ms. Moffly's desk to leave it there, so no one else would step on it.

Then Sydney came back from the bathroom.

She went to Ms. Moffly's desk to put the pass back.

No one opened the snake drawer. But *still*. Sophie could not stand it!

She closed her eyes and wished very hard: *Please! No one else get up.*

Then Archie sneezed again. Sophie was smart this time—she kept her eyes closed. But she could tell from the "Gross!"es and "Ew!"s that green stuff came out again.

"Archie." Ms. Moffly's voice was firmer now. "Please get a tissue from my drawer. I insist," she said.

Archie got up with a groan. Sophie slowly opened her eyes.

Well, she had gotten out of saving Archie one time, but she could not get out of it again. Besides, heroes could not pick and choose. They had to save everyone.

Sophie turned to Kate. She wished that she could wink. But she couldn't, so she just smiled.

Then she crouched on the balls of her feet. She was ready to save Archie when he screamed.

But he did not scream. Or jump. Or even say, "Hey, look at that. It's a snake."

What Archie did was open the desk drawer, take out a tissue, and blow his nose. Hard. Then he closed the drawer and dropped the dirty tissue on the desktop.

"Archie! Put that in the wastepaper basket, please," Ms. Moffly said.

Sophie sat back. Her mouth hung open. How could Archie have missed the bright orange snake in the desk drawer? Were his eyes broken?

Archie shot the tissue into the garbage like a basketball. "Yeah! Three-pointer!" he called.

Nope. Archie's eyes were fine. Which could mean only one thing.

Uh-oh!

The snake was gone!

Ms. Moffly kept reading, but Sophie did not hear a word. She looked around the classroom carefully. Snakes did not just disappear. At least, Sophie did not think so.

Rumplesnakeskin had to be somewhere. But where?

☆　　☆　　☆

"The end," Ms. Moffly said a little while later, closing the book. "Sophie M., what did you think?"

Sophie felt Kate nudge her.

"Hmm?" she murmured. She had been trying to look under the bookcase for a candy-corn-colored snake.

"What did you think of the story?" Ms. Moffly asked again. "Did it surprise you that a mouse could be such a hero?"

"The mouse was a hero?" said Sophie.
Really? Huh. She was sorry she had missed that.

"Oh, Ms. Moffly!" Mindy's hand shot up.

"Yes, Mindy?" said Ms. Moffly.

"I don't think that mouse was *really* a hero," Mindy said. "He didn't save the boy from a *fire*, or anything."

"But he did drive an ambulance," Ben said.

An ambulance? Sophie was *very* sorry she had missed that.

"Well, why don't we go back to our desks and write down what we each think makes a hero," Ms. Moffly said.

She stood up and put the book back on the shelf.

"Let's each make a list and share it," she said. "And remember, a hero can be someone who is very strong or brave. But a hero can also be someone who is very generous, wise, or kind."

Then Ms. Moffly walked to her desk to put away her glasses.

"I know what will be first on my list," Mindy said.

"What?" Lily asked.

"Saving people — or kittens — from fires," Mindy said.

"Oh, mine too," Lily said.

Kate rolled her eyes. Sophie would have, too,

but her eyes were too busy looking around for Rumplesnakeskin.

"Do you know what will be last on my list?" Mindy went on.

"What?" Lily asked.

Mindy looked right at Sophie. "Saving Slinkys," she said.

"Oh, mine too!" Lily agreed.

Sophie glared at Mindy. For a second, she forgot about looking for snakes.

How many times did she have to tell Mindy? She had not saved Slinkys. She had saved a kindergartner. There was a big difference!

But Sophie did not get to tell Mindy that.

Because Ms. Moffly started screaming her head off before Sophie could even open her mouth!

CHAPTER 9

"Agh! Snake!" cried Ms. Moffly. "A snake!"

She was standing frozen by her desk, staring at her chair.

Kate grabbed Sophie's arm. "Ooh! Ms. Moffly screams good, don't you think?" she said.

But that was not what Sophie thought.

The first thing Sophie thought was *Phew. She found Rumplesnakeskin.*

The second thing she thought was *Hey! This is my chance to be a hero again!*

And the third thing she thought was *Oh, no!*

Because before Sophie could move, Toby ran

over and picked Rumplesnakeskin up off the chair!

Ms. Moffly's eyes were big and wide. "Be careful, Toby!" she said.

"Oh, it's okay," he told her. "It's just a corn snake. They don't bite."

Ms. Moffly's face untwisted. A little. "Well, you are still very brave, Toby," she said.

But that was not all she said.

"In fact, I believe you are my hero today!" she added.

Sophie could not believe her ears!

"Yeah, Toby!" the whole class cheered. They began to gather around him and Rumple-snakeskin. Even Kate ran up to see the snake.

Only Sophie stayed back, thinking, *I was supposed to be Ms. Moffly's hero! Those cheers should be for* me, *not Toby!*

How was she going to be Sophie the Hero *now*?

Sophie stood alone in the reading corner, crossing her arms and frowning. Life was not

fair, not when even Toby could be a hero! Why did he have to be such a giant pain?

Sophie almost stomped her foot. She almost did not even want to be a hero now!

Maybe Ms. Moffly was right. Lots of people could be heroes. They could be heroes for all kinds of things, in all kinds of different ways. And maybe being a hero wasn't the best thing for Sophie. Maybe it was better to be something else.

But what?

Oh, poor Rumplesnakeskin! Sophie looked at him and felt bad. She had not meant for him to end up in Toby's yucky hands.

She watched Toby pet the snake's head. "Can we keep it?" Toby asked.

"We can call it Corn Dog!" Archie said.

"Oh, can we hold it? Can we? Please?" a bunch of kids asked.

Ms. Moffly shook her head and held up her hand. "Now, just a minute, class," she said. "This is not a toy. It's a wild animal, remember."

"Uh, I don't know," said Toby. "I think it's a pet."

"A pet?" said Ms. Moffly. "Well, where did it come from?" she asked. She looked a little closer. "You know, this snake looks a lot like Mr. Bloom's new snake," Ms. Moffly said. "I wonder if it is. . . ."

Sophie watched her tap her chin. Sophie was suddenly very nervous. But she was also very impressed. Ms. Moffly was pretty smart for a teacher.

"Toby, you stay there. Everyone else, take a step back," Ms. Moffly said. Then she picked up the phone on the wall by her desk.

"Hello, Mr. Bloom? It's Lila Moffly, in room 10. I was just wondering if maybe you lost a snake."

Sophie watched Ms. Moffly listen for the answer. The teacher bit her lip. Then her eyebrows went up.

"You have?" said Ms. Moffly. "Well, we found one! Yes. It is orange. . . . Where? On my chair . . . Oh, believe me, I'm still shaking! We'll bring it back to you now. I have a brave student holding it right here." Ms. Moffly smiled down at Toby.

Sophie felt like smoke might actually come out of her ears.

Ms. Moffly hung up and looked around the room.

"Well, I was right," she said. "But how in the world did that snake get in here?"

Sophie quickly turned around. She did not want Ms. Moffly to look at her and get any more ideas.

She grabbed a book from the reading shelf. She had read it before. (Twice.) But she opened it and tried to look busy . . . and not guilty at all.

"Sophie?"

She heard Ms. Moffly's voice, but she did not turn around. Besides, Ms. Moffly could have been calling Sophie A., not her.

But Sophie A. was standing near the snake. Which meant that she was standing near Ms. Moffly, too.

Ms. Moffly called, "Sophie," again. This time, it was louder.

Sophie sighed and turned around. Very, very slowly.

"Who? Me?" she said.

"Yes, you, Sophie," said Ms. Moffly.

Sophie swallowed hard. Two times.

CHAPTER 10

Sophie had a feeling in her stomach. It was buzzy, like a beehive. It was spreading to her neck. And it did not feel good at all.

This was something Sophie had not thought of. What if someone asked her how the snake got into room 10? It was bad enough that she had missed her chance to be Ms. Moffly's hero. She really did not want to get in trouble, too.

Ms. Moffly was walking toward her.

"Sophie," she said, "by any chance, do *you* know how the snake got into our room?"

"Um . . . why do you ask?" Sophie said quietly.

She made her eyes really wide so it would look like she had no idea.

"Well," said Ms. Moffly, "you're the only student who does not look surprised to see the snake. And that is a little unusual. Since the snake came from your sister's classroom, I thought that I would ask you."

"Oh," said Sophie. Ms. Moffly had a point.

"So?" said Ms. Moffly.

"So," Sophie repeated.

She knew what she should say: "Nope. I do not know!" That would be so easy.

But it was not easy. Not when she looked up at Ms. Moffly. It was like looking at her mom or dad. Lying to them was hard, and it never worked out as she hoped.

Sophie looked at the floor. Then at the ceiling. Then out the window. Then she looked back at Ms. Moffly.

"I took him and brought him here," she said with a sigh.

The whole class said, "Ah!"

Then "Oh!"

Then "Ooh!"

"I knew it!" said Mindy.

"Me too!" Lily added.

"Why'd you go to all that trouble and just leave it on a chair?" Toby asked.

"Quiet, class. Why did you bring the snake here, Sophie?" Ms. Moffly asked.

Oh, not that question! And not with everyone staring.

Sophie wished she were getting a shot at the doctor. Or sitting in the audience at one of her sister's boring ballet recitals. Anywhere else in the world would be better, really.

How could she tell Ms. Moffly (and the whole class) that she took Rumplesnakeskin so that she could be a hero again?

Ms. Moffly put her hand on Sophie's shoulder. "Was it because you wanted our class to have a snake?" she asked.

"Um . . ." Sophie thought about that. "Kind of," she said.

In a way, she did.

Ms. Moffly nodded. "I understand. You know, I've thought about getting a pet for our class." She glanced at Rumplesnakeskin and shivered. "But never a snake!"

"Really?" said Kate and Eve and Mia and a few other kids in the class.

"Really," Ms. Moffly said.

"How about a bearded dragon?" Archie suggested.

"Oh, yeah!" said Toby. "I love it when they eat crickets and spit out the legs!"

"I was thinking maybe guppies," said Ms. Moffly. "Or a bunny. But we'll see."

A bunny! Sophie perked up. How fun would that be?

But then Ms. Moffly's eyes were on her again. Her stomach bees started buzzing.

"Sophie," said Ms. Moffly. "I think you know that taking a snake is not a minor infraction."

Sophie nodded. Yes. She did know that. Whatever that meant.

"And there will be consequences," Ms. Moffly went on.

Consequences. *Ugh!* Sophie knew that word, unfortunately.

"Tomorrow you will stay in at recess and do extra math," Ms. Moffly said.

The bees in Sophie's stomach settled down a bit. She hated to miss recess. But math? She kind of liked that.

Ms. Moffly smiled and folded her hands.

"Still, I want to commend you for your honesty, Sophie. I'm proud of you for that," Ms. Moffly said. "It is important to tell the truth. Always."

Suddenly, all the bees in Sophie's stomach flew away. And what they left felt like warm honey. It spread to the tips of her toes and her hands.

Sophie *was* honest—about taking the snake, anyway—and it felt good. Almost as good as being a hero!

"Now, I think you should return the snake to Mr. Bloom," Ms. Moffly said. "I want you to tell him what happened, and that it will never happen again."

"No problem." Sophie nodded. Then she crossed her heart. "I will tell the truth. The whole truth. And nothing but the truth," she said.

"Very good," Ms. Moffly said with a smile.

Then Sophie remembered Hayley's jacket. She had hung it on her hook. She ran over and grabbed it. She could take it to Hayley and tell the truth about that, too!

She put the jacket over one arm and walked up to Toby.

"I'll take Rumplesnakeskin now," she said, holding out her arms.

"Here you go," he said. He handed the snake over and stuck out his tongue.

Sophie stuck her tongue out, too. Very quickly. Like Rumplesnakeskin.

"Oh, and for the record, I did not leave him on the chair. I put him in a drawer and he crawled out," she said.

Sophie smiled at Rumplesnakeskin. *Humph!*

Toby thought he was a hero. Anyone could hold a snake. But could anyone tell the truth? All the time? About everything? That was the question!

And Sophie knew the answer — she could. And she would.

She would be Sophie the Honest from now on!

She smiled down at the sticky *H* on her shirt. She didn't even have to change her shirt to fit her new name!

(But yeah, she should probably wash it.)

So maybe SOPHIE the HERO
isn't the perfect name.

But SOPHIE isn't giving up yet!

SOPHIE
the
CHATTERBOX

by Lara Bergen

SCHOLASTIC

Take a peek at Sophie's next adventure....

They felt the bus lurch forward. A round of "On Top of Spaghetti" started up. But Sophie and Kate did not sing. Sophie was tired of that song, for one thing. Plus, she had some more Sophie the Honest stuff to tell Kate.

"So guess what. I told my mom and dad about taking the fifth-grade's snake yesterday. And that was before my big sister, Hayley, could say anything," Sophie said.

Kate looked a little surprised. And a lot impressed.

"Did you get in big trouble?" Kate asked Sophie.

Sophie grinned and shook her head.

"No! That's the best part," she said. "My mom

and dad were so proud of me for being honest. They didn't punish me or anything!"

And that was not all Sophie had told her parents the night before. She also told them about the squash stuck to the bottom of the dinner table. (By her. Every time they had squash for dinner.)

"You know, it honestly feels good not to have secrets!" Sophie told Kate.

"Wow!" Kate said. "And how about your basement? Did you tell them why it stinks? That we were making potions, and that it wasn't your little brother?"

"Oh...that," Sophie said. She had forgotten about that. Almost. "I haven't told them about that yet," she said.

"Well, how about your mom's stockings? The ones we played fashion show with? Did you tell her Tiptoe didn't rip them? Did you tell her we did?" Kate asked.

"Er...no," Sophie said. And she did not really

want to. Tiptoe was her kitten. She could not really get in trouble. But Sophie sure could.

Still . . .

"I'll tell them," she told Kate. "I will! I promise!"

From now on, Sophie would be completely, totally honest. After all, that was who she was now!